This book belongs to

....

For Mr Roger Bear,
much love— J.N.

EGMONT

We bring stories to life

First published in Great Britain 2011
by Egmont UK Limited
239 Kensington High Street, London W8 6SA

Text and illustrations copyright © Jill Newton 2011
The moral rights of the author/illustrator
have been asserted

ISBN 978 14052 4965 2 (Hardback)
ISBN 978 14052 4966 9 (Paperback)

10 9 8 7 6 5 4 3 2 1

A CIP catalogue record for this title
is available from the British Library

Printed and bound in Singapore

DON'T WAKE MR BEAR!

Jill Newton

EGMONT

Down in the wood,
between two oak trees,
a golden leaf

floated

to the

ground.

Ting!

Dormouse struck his triangle.
He was the leader of the Woodland Orchestra
and it was time for the lullaby of the forest to begin.

Dormouse gathered the orchestra together.
"Places, please," he said.

The squirrels sat in their trees
and blew the sound of the breeze.

Plink plonk plink!

The wood pigs tapped their xylophones and the acorns dropped from the trees.

Thrrrrrrrrrrum!

The rabbits strummed their harps as the leaves fluttered down around them.

**And, remember,
WHATEVER you do,
don't wake Mr Bear!"**

With that he went off to bed.

The gentle music was making
everyone, and everything,
feel very sleepy.

Until ...

Suddenly . . .

BANG!!

A carload of **wolves** crashed into a tree.

"HOWDY!" called one wolf,
tooting his horn.

"DO YOU WANT A PARTY?"
yelled another.

"Shhhh!" whispered
the squirrels.
"Be quiet! You'll wake
Mr Bear!"

But the wolves weren't listening.

Out of the car came
the wolves' **drums,**
    and their **lights,**
        and their **speakers.**

"Go away!" begged the rabbits.
"You'll wake Mr Bear!"

"We don't care
about a silly
old bear!"
sang the wolves.

Before long,
the **squirrels** and the **rabbits**
and the **wood pigs** didn't care
about **Mr Bear** either.

They were having
MUCH too
much fun!

Until …

RO

"Uh-oh," said the squirrels.
"It's time for you to go!"

"You've woken
Mr Bear!"
said the rabbits.

"But we're
on holiday!"
protested
the wolves.

Mr Bear turned
towards the animals ...

"Don't be ridiculous!"
he said to them.
"If these chaps are on holiday,
we must show them a good time!"

Mr Bear grabbed a snazzy-looking shirt
and led the party,
    dancing and stomping through
the forest all night,
    creating the loudest
        rumpus of all.

The sun had just started to rise **when . . .**

...there was a sudden

CRASH!

The party animals stopped
in their tracks.

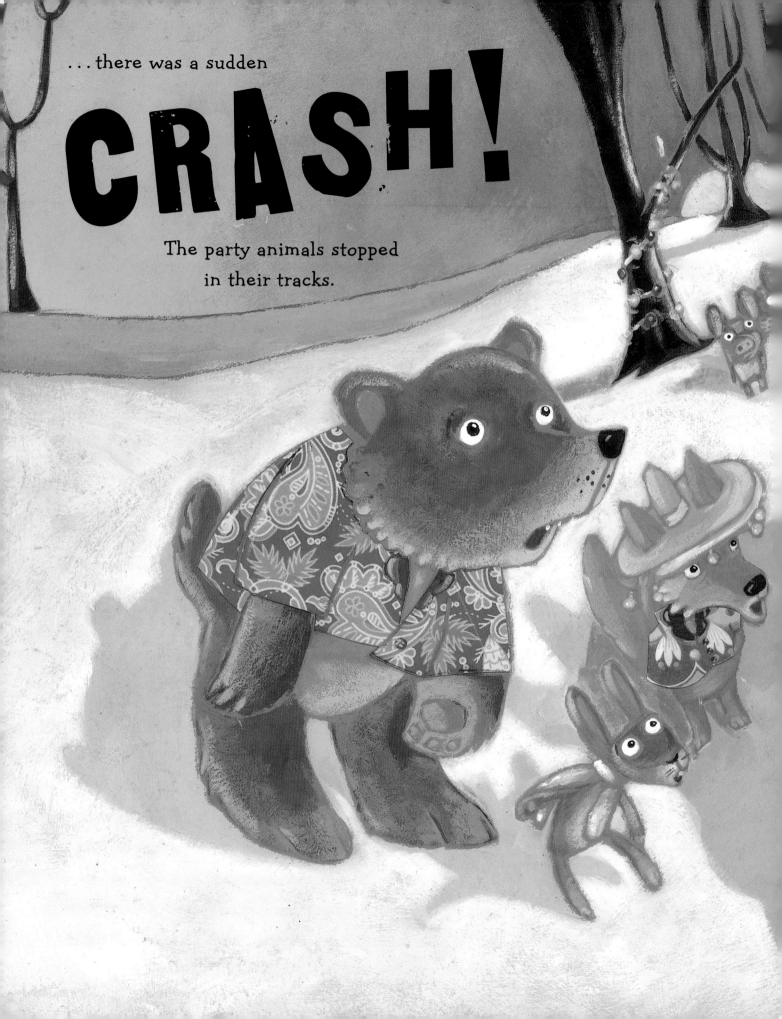

There stood a very **tired**

and very **angry** . . .

. . . Dormouse!

"WHAT DID I TELL YOU NOT TO DO?"

he yelled at the rabbits.

"You told us not to
wake Mr Bear,"
they replied.

**"AND WHAT HAVE
YOU DONE?"**
he yelled at the squirrels.

"Woken Mr Bear," they said meekly.

**"AND WHAT
MADE YOU
WAKE MR BEAR?"**

The squirrels and rabbits
waited for the wolves to explain –
but the wolves were
nowhere to be seen.

Mr Bear bumbled over.
"Great timing little fellow.
Where's the food?
I'm feeling peckish."

"**FOOD!**
There **IS** no food,
you silly bear!
The forest is going to sleep,
just like you should be.
Without rest, the trees won't
grow any berries or nuts.
There'll be **NO** juicy bugs
to pick on. And how would
you feel then?" Dormouse shouted.

"Not very happy," mumbled Mr Bear.

"SO BE QUIET THEN AND GO TO BED!" shouted Dormouse.

Ting!

Dormouse struck his triangle.
The squirrels climbed up into their trees,
the wood pigs tapped their xylophones
and the rabbits picked up their harps.

The Woodland Orchestra played
the lullaby of the forest once more,
as Mr Bear yawned
and shuffled back off to his cave.

"**Perfect,**" yawned Dormouse.
"**Perfect music for the long winter sleep. Just one more thing . . .**"

He turned to the wolves, hiding up in the trees.
"**I'd like you lot to keep time, but quietly!**

After all,
YOU DON'T WANT TO WAKE MR DORMOUSE,
do you?"